The Know It All Kitty Dreams of His Mom

Kathy Jernigan

and

Karen McCarty, MS

Order this book online at www.trafford.com
or email orders@trafford.com

Most Trafford titles are also available at major online book retailers.

 www.trafford.com

North America & international
toll-free: 844 688 6899 (USA & Canada)
fax: 812 355 4082

Our mission is to efficiently provide the world's finest, most comprehensive book publishing
service, enabling every author to experience success. To find out how to publish your book,
your way, and have it available worldwide, visit us online at www.trafford.com

ISBN: 978-1-6987-0994-9 (sc)
ISBN: 978-1-6987-0993-2 (e)

Library of Congress Control Number: 2021921731

Print information available on the last page.

Trafford rev. 11/18/2021

This book is dedicated to Carole Backus, a talented artist and beautiful human, whose illustrations full of creativity and energy brought the Know It All Kitty to life once again. Her amazing artwork and well established love of cats shines through in this book. Rest in peace dear friend.

Once upon a time there was a sassy yellow cat that lived in the forest. His friends called him the Know It All Kitty because he thought he knew everything.

But one day, he just couldn't figure things out. He was sleeping in his little cave. He was dreaming of his Mother who died when he was a small kitten. He was afraid he was forgetting her.

"I'll go see my friend Molly. Maybe she can help," he said.

When she opened the door, Molly Kitty saw the look on his face and asked him,

"Did you have your sad dream again?"

"Yes," he said.

"I think you need to go see Tree Wizard and tell him about your dream," said Molly. "I'll go with you."

The Know It All Kitty frowned. "That won't help."

"You'll see," said Molly.

"Come on!"

"How do you know which tree is the wizard? They all look alike," the Know It All Kitty grumbled.

"Oh," said Molly, "you can tell by the blue birds."

And Molly was right. Tree Wizard was the biggest tree in the forest and dozens of blue birds flew in and out of his branches. He seemed to be sleeping when they arrived. Long twig eyelashes twitched on his face.

"What's that sound?" said the Know It All Kitty.

"I think he's snoring," said Molly.

"Not anymore" . . .
said the Tree wizard.

6

"My friend Molly wants me to tell you my dream about my Mom," said the Know It All Kitty, secretly wanting to run away to his cave.

"Oh, Molly is right. Dreams are very important! My name is Tree Wizard and listening to dreams is part of my job."

"But Tree Wizard," said the Know It All Kitty, "it was a sad dream and I keep having it over and over. What good are sad dreams?"

Tree Wizard's big brown eyes sparkled.

"A dream you have many times is special. I want you to sit down in front of my trunk and tell the whole story, so the words of your dream fly up into my branches."

The Know It All Kitty felt so grouchy and angry at having to tell his dream again. "I don't want to keep saying something that makes me so sad," he argued.

The Know It All Kitty crossed his arms over his chest.

HRRRRRRRRMMMMMMMMMMMMMPPPPPHHHHHHHHH!!!!

"Every time you tell a dream you get closer to the gifts it has for you," said Tree Wizard.

After a long time, when the Know It All Kitty had said all the words of his dream, Tree Wizard's eyes closed.

Molly whispered to the Know It All Kitty, "Is Tree Wizard asleep?"
Before he could answer, a swishing sound rushed over them.
At first, they thought the tree was snoring again.

But the wind gusted and blew hard. It sounded like a storm coming, and they were scared.

"Run inside my trunk, I'll keep you safe," Tree Wizard shouted.

The Know it all Kitty and Molly looked at each other and wondered what to do, but the wind howled louder so they ran inside.

They were surprised to find warm cozy blankets and a little table set with peanut butter cookies and two bowls of milk. By the time they finished their cookies and milk, the wind was quiet outside.

Tree Wizard smiled and said, "The bluebirds heard your dream and they always know what you need when you're sad. They brought you some gifts. If you climb up into my branches, you'll find them hidden in the leaves."

The Know It All Kitty and Molly began climbing, sinking their sharp claws into Tree Wizard's bark.

Tree Wizard chuckled, "Don't worry, your claws don't hurt, they tickle," he laughed.

The Know It All Kitty crept out onto a long branch and pushed his paw deep into the leaves. He felt something soft. He pulled it out and found a red velvet bag. When he opened it, there was a picture of his Mom Kitty holding him in her mouth.

By the time he and Molly climbed the whole tree, they had collected five velvet bags. In the first one was the picture of his Mother holding him. In the second was the collar his Mother wore. It was pink leather, with some of her soft fur, just like his, caught in the buckle. In the third velvet bag were two shiny green stones just the color of Mom Kitty's eyes. In the fourth bag was a tattered catnip mouse that Mom Kitty had given him when he was born.

But the last bag was empty.

"Why is this one empty?" asked the Know It All Kitty?"

"Put your nose inside," said Tree Wizard. "Sniff!"

So the Know It All Kitty sniffed inside the bag and suddenly he could feel his mother licking him clean with her rough tongue. Her purring filled his body. He could hear her meowing to call him for supper and smell the sweetness of her soft fur.

"The last bag isn't empty at all. It's full of all the best things about Mom," he said.

"Every time you see a bluebird," Tree Wizard said, "take a deep breathe and soon you will find those memories of your Mom Kitty are deep inside you. They will never disappear," he explained.

Tree Wizard smiled so wide some of his bark cracked and fell off, frightening a baby bluebird.

Then Tree Wizard patted the kitties with one of his leafy branches and told them it was his naptime.

Molly and the Know it all Kitty were feeling sleepy too so they settled down next to Tree Wizard and fell fast asleep.

Whenever the Know it all Kitty felt sad about his Mom kitty, he remembered all he had learned from Tree Wizard. He keeps the velvet bag in a special place just for those sad times to remind him that Mom Kitty is always with him.

Printed in the United States
by Baker & Taylor Publisher Services